Commander Gander

goes to

Commander Gander

goes to

COME FROM AWAY

Written and Illustrated by Dawn Baker

PENNYWELL BOOKS

ST. JOHN'S

Library and Archives Canada Cataloguing in Publication

Title: Commander Gander goes to Come from away / written and illustrated by Dawn Baker.
Names: Baker, Dawn, 1962- author, illustrator.
Identifiers: Canadiana (print) 20190066369 | Canadiana (ebook) 20190066385 | ISBN 9781771177238
  (softcover) | ISBN 9781771177245 (PDF)
Classification: LCC PS8603.A453 C66 2019 | DDC jC813/.6—dc23

© 2019 by Dawn Baker

PRINTED IN CANADA

This paper has been certified to meet the environmental and social standards of the Forest Stewardship Council® (FSC®) and comes from responsibly managed forests, and verified recycled sources.

Pennywell Books is an imprint of Flanker Press Limited.

FLANKER PRESS LTD.
PO BOX 2522, STATION C
ST. JOHN'S, NL A1C 6K1 CANADA

TELEPHONE: (709) 739-4477   TOLL-FREE: 1-866-739-4420   FAX: (709) 739-4420

WWW.FLANKERPRESS.COM

9 8 7 6 5 4 3 2 1

Cover Design: Graham Blair
Interior Layout: Peter Hanes

 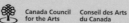

We acknowledge the [financial] support of the Government of Canada. *Nous reconnaissons l'appui [financier] du gouvernement du Canada.* We acknowledge the support of the Canada Council for the Arts, which last year invested $153 million to bring the arts to Canadians throughout the country. *Nous remercions le Conseil des arts du Canada de son soutien. L'an dernier, le Conseil a investi 153 millions de dollars pour mettre de l'art dans la vie des Canadiennes et des Canadiens de tout le pays.* We acknowledge the financial support of the Government of Newfoundland and Labrador, Department of Tourism, Culture and Recreation for our publishing activities.

I would like to dedicate this book to first responders everywhere.

Thank you for all that you do.

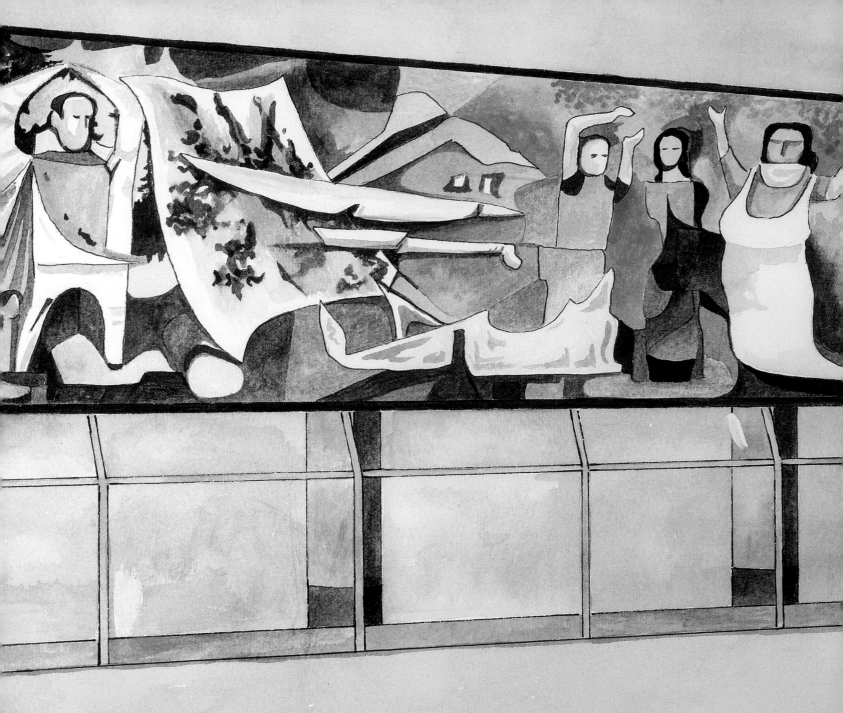

Commander Gander was so excited he could hardly sit still. He was at the airport in the town of Gander, the place that gave him his name. Soon he would be on his way to New York City!

The Commander worked for the town of Gander, which was built around the airport. It was a place where about 10,000 people lived in the middle of the island of Newfoundland. He was called on to help with special events in the town, especially when children were involved. Commander Gander loved his job!

Way back in September of 2001, some bad things happened in New York City and other places in America. On that sad day, many planes carrying almost 7,000 passengers had to land at Gander Airport. Some of those travellers were children, and they had to stay in Gander for days.

The people from Gander and other small towns in central Newfoundland did everything they could to help the stranded passengers. The Newfoundlanders opened their homes and their hearts to the people from the planes. They made sure everyone had lots to eat, clean clothes, somewhere to sleep, and someone to talk to and comfort them.

Commander Gander was busier than ever. He knew the children from the planes were unhappy, so he did everything he could to make them feel better. The Commander played and danced and acted silly, and he even hosted a party with clowns, cakes, and balloons!

Sometimes the Commander just sat quietly with the children and their families. He did his very best.

The unexpected visitors from the planes were in Gander for five days. Then, at last, they were told it was safe to leave and continue their journeys. When they were all back in their own homes, they began to tell stories to their friends and families about the kindness they had received in Newfoundland. In time, these stories became very well-known.

Two very special people, David Hein and Irene Sankoff, heard the stories and began to write down the wonderful things they were told about Gander. These stories became an amazing musical show called *Come From Away*. David and Irene created it to help people everywhere remember the kindness that the "plane people" had been shown.

Much to the surprise of everyone in Gander, and all of Newfoundland, *Come From Away* was a huge hit on Broadway in New York City.

And now Commander Gander was about to go and see what it was all about!

At last, he arrived in New York City! Everywhere there was such hustle and bustle, colour and movement, and every sort of sound and smell. He loved it all!

The first thing the Commander did was pick up his ticket for *Come From Away*.

Next he decided to go sightseeing. Commander Gander took a tour on a special bus and visited the Statue of Liberty and the Empire State Building.

He bought a hot dog from a street cart and got
T-shirts for all his friends back home.

Commander Gander made sure to slow down and spend time at the 9/11 Memorial. Standing there and looking on, with his hat held in his wings, his eyes filled with tears.

Soon it was time to go see the musical. The Commander had been so busy in New York he was almost late! He got to his seat just before the lights dimmed and the music started.

While watching the show, Commander Gander remembered those days in 2001. He thought about the day when the children were leaving on buses to go back to the planes. It didn't seem that long ago, but they would all be grown-ups now, maybe with children of their own. He hoped they were all doing well.

All too soon, *Come From Away* was over. The applause was very loud! The Commander jumped to his feet and clapped and cheered along with everyone else.

Then, someone close by recognized him. A girl squealed, "I can't believe it! You are Commander Gander! You were there! You helped all of those people!"

Suddenly, people from the audience surrounded the Commander! They wanted to shake his wing and take pictures with him. He felt embarrassed and full of pride at the same time! Of course, he knew he was only one of the thousands of people who did their very best to help.

Commander Gander even got to meet some of the cast members of the musical! They seemed to be just as impressed by him as he was by them. It was a magical and very strange feeling.

The next day, the Commander was on an airplane heading back home. As he looked out the window, he thought about everything that had happened, especially the thanks he had received for helping out during 9/11.

The Commander knew deep inside that he didn't do it for praise. Like so many others, he helped because it was the right thing to do. Helping others always is. Commander Gander promised that was one thing he would never forget.

In addition to Gander, the following neighbouring communities in central Newfoundland also opened their hearts and homes to the "plane people" and deserve recognition:

Appleton
Gambo
Glenwood
Lewisporte
Norris Arm

A special thank you to the writers of *Come From Away*

Irene Sankoff and David Hein

and to

Max Grossman

along with

Randy Adams
Kenny Alhadeff
Marleen Alhadeff
Beowulf Boritt
Petrina Bromley
Heather Cloud
Jenn Colella

Romano Di Nillo
Meghan Dixon
Alana Duthie
Mayor Percy Farwell
Sue Frost
Seth Glewen
Carl Pasbjerg

Marshall Purdy
Neil J. Rosini
Alex Stone
Abbie Strassler
Lauren Tucker
Daniel M. Wasser
Brian Williams

Special thanks to: Abrams Artists Agency; Alchemy Production Group; Franklin, Weinrib, Rudell and Vassallo, PC; Junkyard Dog Productions; Kiss the Cod Broadway LP; and On the Rialto

Dawn Baker has been a visual artist and children's writer since 1992. A graduate of Memorial University with a bachelor of education and a certificate in library studies, she has served on the board of directors of The Rooms since 2006. In 2015, Dawn served as a juror for the Governor General's Literary Awards and toured Ontario as part of TD Canadian Children's Book Week.

Over 100,000 books sold!

ALSO BY DAWN BAKER

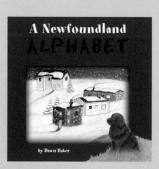

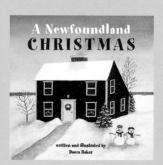

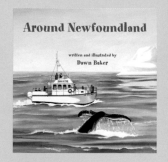

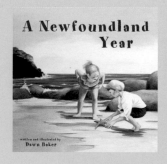
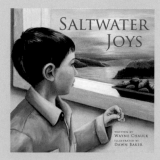

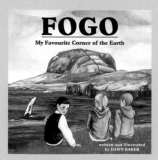